DOOMSDAY LASER

MISSION 1

MAX CRAVEN

First published in Great Britain in 1997
by Reed Books Children's Publishing
Michelin House, 81 Fulham Road, London SW3 6RB
and Auckland and Melbourne

ISBN 0-7497-3170-2

1 3 5 7 9 10 8 6 4 2

Printed in the UK by Cox & Wyman Ltd

CONTENTS

NIGHT PATROL

Two o'clock in the morning and the city streets of mighty Centropolis were almost quiet.

From out of the shadows came a lone figure on a powerful motorbike. Dressed in black leather, he was almost invisible in the dark of the night, as he weaved his way among the buildings of glass that towered over him. Only the narrow beam of light from the bike's headlamp pierced the gloom.

Who is this mysterious rider and why does he patrol the city streets while everyone else sleeps? He has a name, but he has forgotten it. He has a past too, but his memories of it are lost forever. For now, he calls himself Action Man, and tonight he makes sure the streets are safe.

As the mighty black bike passed by, a pile of rubbish bins on the side of the road began to shake. But when Action Man was half a kilometre down the street, the bins were still vibrating, moved by some force other than that of the powerful bike.

Something was wrong. Action Man's canny sixth sense warned him of danger, so he slowed the bike to a crawl. There was a strange burning smell in the air and then a foul, grey smoke blotted out the light from the bike's lamp. Action Man was about to alert the fire services when, suddenly, the ground beneath his bike swelled and pulsed. A great, tearing noise ripped through the air and Action Man was thrown from the bike. He quickly scrambled to his feet and ran across the road, dodging falling steel beams and shattered glass.

With lightning reflexes, Action Man smashed head-first through the plate-glass window of a shop, as massive concrete blocks crashed onto the road behind him.

From inside the shop, he watched as the building opposite collapsed into a pile of rubble, throwing deadly missiles of glass and steel down the road. For what seemed like hours, the sound of tearing metal filled the air until, finally, all was quiet.

Action Man walked cautiously out onto the street. Harmless dust and particles now fell gently around him. What could have caused this? An earthquake? But how could an earthquake hit only one building and leave all the rest standing? Action Man walked to where the collapsed building had once stood; all that remained was a smoking pile of twisted metal.

He clambered up the pile of rubble, his quick eyes searching for clues. Action Man made his way over to where the smoke was thickest. It was coming from a huge crater in the middle of the rubble. As he leaned carefully over the edge, he was struck by the intense heat rising from the hole. Peering through the smoke, he saw that the bottom of the crater was glowing white-hot.

"This looks evil," whispered Action Man to himself.

The wail of sirens in the distance broke his train of thought. He scrambled down to the road and located his bike. He checked it over carefully and found the damage was only minor. But that wasn't surprising; this was no ordinary bike. Action Man wiped the dust from the Team X-Treme logo on the bike's petrol tank and started the engine. He had to contact Station X-Treme fast. This collapsing building looked like the work of one man—the one man Action Man has spent his entire waking life fighting—Doctor X.

Circling high above the earth's atmosphere, Space Station X-Treme lay shielded from detection by a special scrambler code. Deep inside the station's interior, Natalie Poole, ex-British intelligence agent, and communications expert, was woken from a deep sleep by the stop-start beeping sound of the incoming report alert. She climbed out of her bunk and walked into the main control room, switching the receive module to unscramble. Instantly, the image of Action Man appeared on the giant screen mounted above the control desk.

"Good evening, Natalie," he said, smiling.

"Good morning, you mean," snorted Natalie. "What's up?"

"Trouble in Centropolis," said Action Man, dropping the smile. "Major office block collapsed in the middle of the night."

"Well, it can't have been an earthquake," mused Natalie, rubbing the sleep from her eyes, "we would have picked up the seismology report."

"No, it wasn't an earthquake. This building went down solo."

"Explosion?"

"No," said Action Man. "No explosion. . .but definitely some sort of sabotage."

"Doctor X," hissed Natalie.

"More than likely."

There was a loud crash behind Natalie. She turned to see Knuck Williams, American ex-marine and explosives wizard, shuffle into the room, yawning.

"What in blazes is going on?" he boomed. "Waking a man from his sleep. . .oh, Action Man. Didn't realise it was you."

Action Man quickly filled Knuck in on the situation.

"And you say there was no explosion?" asked Knuck.

"That's right. But there was a strange crater in the middle of the rubble, glowing white-hot. Any ideas?"

"Oh, I've got ideas," said Knuck, "plenty of them. But they won't mean anything until I get down there and have a look for myself."

"Okay," said Action Man, "make it fast."

Knuck ran from the room to prepare for the descent to earth, as Action Man grinned to himself.

"What are you grinning at?" asked Natalie.

"I never realised how cheerful Knuck is when he's woken from his beauty sleep," he said, laughing.

"Go easy on him," smiled Natalie. "He was up all night with the United Nations Security Council."

"General Norris giving him a hard time?"

"Poor Knuck. With you away on earth patrol, he's had to do all the budget reports for Team X-Treme. And you know how much he hates doing sums."

"I'll go easy on him when he lands," said Action Man. "Listen, Natalie, when Jacques wakes, ask him to do a check on the electricity grids for Centropolis and any other big city. Whoever's doing this must be using a massive source of energy."

"Will do," said Natalie, looking back at the team's sleeping quarters, where Jacques' wheelchair was leaning against his bunk.

Jacques Duprey, a sixteen-year-old computer genius, was capable of tapping into any computer system in the world.

Natalie turned back to look into Action Man's eyes; they were so deep and unfathomable. She often found herself wondering what he was thinking, how he felt about his past—a past that was stolen from him by Doctor X's mind-destruction serum. She knows it troubles him, that he wishes he knew his history. But she also knows that he would never admit that to anyone.

And now Doctor X is back, she thought, wreaking havoc in the city of Centropolis. But not for long. Not if Team X-Treme has anything to do with it.

KNUCK INVESTIGATES

The city of Centropolis lay sprawled beneath Knuck Williams as he guided Jet X-Treme towards the military airport. He could see the huge hole left by the collapsed building, emergency service crews racing around like ants, and billows of grey smoke still rising from the rubble. He was keen to get down there and investigate. The explosive hadn't been made that Knuck couldn't detect; and by the look of this mess, the villains had definitely used explosives.

As Jet X-Treme glided onto the tarmac, Knuck wondered about Action Man's uncanny ability to locate trouble. Ever since Action Man had appeared out of nowhere to join Team X-Treme, and eventually to lead it, Knuck had admired him. His quick mind in a crisis, his skill at climbing, fighting, running. . . everything. And then, of course, there was his strange knack of being where the action was; perhaps that's why the name Action Man had stuck so well. He'd only arrived at Centropolis last night, and already buildings were falling down around his ears.

Knuck opened the jet's hatch and was greeted immediately by an impatient Action Man.

"This way," he barked, pointing to the Team X-Treme jeep parked nearby.

Knuck climbed down and ran to the jeep after Action Man. They drove quickly to the site of destruction; fire crews and rescue vehicles surrounded the area. Knuck was instantly struck by the smell of the smoke that erupted from the rubble every few seconds. The long, grey plume looked like it was coming out of a volcano, but Knuck knew there was nothing natural or majestic about this smoke. This was man-made and dirty.

"What do you make of it, Knuck?" asked Action Man, leaning against the steering wheel.

"That smell," muttered Knuck, "it's like nothing I've ever encountered."

"I was afraid of that," said Action Man. Whatever they've used is new and powerful."

Knuck climbed out of the jeep and set up a small, black box by the side of the rubble. He drew out a long, silver antenna, then detached a flimsy sheet of transparent plastic from the bottom of the box. Waving the plastic through the air, Knuck watched the dials on the black box keenly, hoping for some sort of reaction.

"Nothing," he muttered. "No traces of TNT, plastic explosives, nuclear devices. . .you name it. Just nothing!" He put the sheet of plastic back under the box and pushed the antenna down again.

"Come with me," said Action Man, climbing to the top of the rubble.

Rescue teams were searching the area with sensitive listening devices, hoping to locate any survivors, but it appeared the building had been empty when it collapsed.

"At least no-one was hurt," said Knuck, as he reached the top.

"Yes," mused Action Man. "But I've got a bad feeling that it won't stop at this."

"I've got the same feeling, friend," said Knuck, leaning over the edge of the crater Action Man had discovered the night before. He whistled slowly when he saw the pool of molten metal and rock that lay at the bottom.

"What do you think?" asked Action Man.

"It would take a tremendous force to create such heat," muttered Knuck. "Tonnes and tonnes of TNT, something nuclear. . .but it's not that."

"All we know for sure," said Action Man briskly, "is that this building didn't fall down by itself. This was definitely sabotage."

"I suggest we split up," said Knuck. "Whatever caused this is not going to be easy to hide, even in a big city like Centropolis."

"Good idea," said Action Man. "You take the jeep, I'll patrol on the bike. We've got to stop this fast. Get in touch with Natalie and Jacques; tell them to be prepared to join us here if necessary."

Then he was gone, down the side of the rubble and onto his bike. Knuck wasted no time in following. Team X-Treme had work to do.

A CLOSE CALL

How do you patrol when you don't even know what you are looking for?

This question nagged at Action Man as he cruised the deserted streets of Centropolis.

The people of the city were staying indoors tonight, fearful that another building might go down. As far as Action Man was concerned, there was no "might" about it. The destruction would be repeated, especially if Doctor X was behind it.

He pulled the bike over and listened; perhaps the noises of the night would provide a clue. He heard nothing out of the ordinary: the hum of distant traffic, dogs barking.

A short "beep" sounded from his communicator and Action Man switched it on.

"Nothing to report," said Knuck. "Just thought I'd check up on your progress."

"Same as you, I'm afraid," said Action Man. "Still . . .I don't know. . ."

"What is it?" asked Knuck.

"Just a feeling. Make contact again in half an hour."

He switched the communicator off and started up

his bike. Action Man couldn't account for this strange sixth sense he had, this ability to predict danger. He thought it could have something to do with his loss of memory; it could be a side-effect of Doctor X's mind-destruction serum. Or maybe he had it before, in that past he can't remember. Action Man shook his head, there was work to do now, the past would have to wait for another day.

He turned into a dark alley-way, unsure of what was leading him into it.

Something was here, but what? Then he saw it, a dull, red glow against the wall. It was so slight that an ordinary person might have missed it. Action Man was about to stop the bike when a flash of danger raced through his head. He revved the bike up to full throttle, kicking back onto the rear wheel for a split second before hitting the road at top speed. A brick wall loomed in front of him and Action Man hit the brake hard. The bike skidded sideways and the smell of burning rubber came up off the road. The bike came to a halt in front of the wall and Action Man looked around to see the ground behind him glow red-hot, then white, before becoming a pool of molten bitumen and rock. Giant sparks flew from the volcano-like hole and exploded against the walls of the alley.

It won't take whoever did that long to realise they missed me, thought Action Man. He quickly started back down the alley, but the way was blocked by molten metal and flying sparks. The only way out was through the wall. He turned the bike around to face the wall and activated a switch on the handlebars. A small missile emerged from the side of the fuel tank, and Action Man placed his feet firmly on the ground to steady the bike. He pointed the front of the bike at the middle of the wall, then armed the missile. As he waited for the firing sequence to finish, Action Man became aware of voices above him. He could just make out the words, "there he is, near the wall." There wasn't a moment to lose.

A small red light flashed on the handlebars; all systems were go. Action Man pressed the fire button. The bike kicked slightly as the missile shot from its port. It slammed into the wall and the brick and mortar of the wall evaporated into powder, leaving a rough hole for Action Man to exit through. He threw the bike into turbo; it jolted violently, then sped through the hole, just as another deadly ray hit the ground behind him.

As he sped down the highway, Action Man thought about what had happened. It told him two things. First, Doctor X was definitely behind the sabotage. The attack in the alley was deliberate, and the only person who would have been able to identify him so readily was X. Second, it told him how the building might have gone down last night, but he'd save that idea for Knuck.

He turned off the highway and headed back towards the city. He immediately became aware of the smell of burning metal. The thundering boom in the distance only confirmed what he already knew: another building was going down.

STREET FIGHTING

In the makeshift Team X-Treme headquarters, Natalie and Jacques worked quickly on a communications system for Centropolis. The chaos of the previous night had almost brought the great city to its knees; only quick intervention on the part of Team X-Treme and the authorities had averted disaster. Three buildings went down after the attack on Action Man: the telecommunications centre, the police headquarters and the major bank computer centre.

After arriving from Station X-Treme, Natalie had worked through the night and all day to establish some form of communications for the police and emergency services. She had finished the last piece of wiring half an hour ago, and now wanted to test the system. She zoned in on a police patrol that was in the centre of the city and buzzed them.

"Hello?" came a fuzzy voice. "Who is this?"

"It's Central Command," snapped Natalie. "Who did you think it would be? I'm testing the emergency communications system."

"Well, you're coming through loud and clear, mam."

"You can address me as Colonel Poole, officer."

"Yes, sir. . .I mean, mam. . .I mean. . ."

"Anything to report from your area?" sighed Natalie.

"Well, we have an unconfirmed report that a large gang is heading this way. . . apparently they are armed."

"Do you need reinforcements?" asked Natalie.

"We're not taking it that seriously—"

The line crackled for a second, a loud bang erupted from the speakers and then everything went quiet.

"Sounds pretty serious to me," muttered Natalie. She called for reinforcements to the area.

Centropolis is in chaos, thought Natalie, as she walked over to where Jacques was working. And that's exactly what Doctor X wants. If he can destroy this great city, make it a ruin where gangs roam free and the police are powerless, then he will have shown his strength to the world. And he won't stop at Centropolis. How many other large cities will he destroy before the governments of the world meet his demands?

Jacques was wearing his virtual reality mask. Anyone looking at him might think he was playing a game. He swayed from side to side in his wheelchair, sometimes muttering to himself, sometimes uttering short commands such as "yes" or "turn left and continue." Natalie, however, knew better; with his genius and a virtual reality mask, Jacques could enter any computer system and recover information. And information was just as important as weapons in the war against Doctor X.

There was no point in interrupting the boy now, thought Natalie; what she had to say could wait. The next step was to contact Knuck and Action Man and alert them to the news about the gangs. Something told her they would probably know already, especially Action Man. That's just the way he was.

Action Man, dressed in his street combat guise, crouched beside a tall building. He was watching a group of suspicious characters on the other side of the road. He'd been expecting this sort of thing: criminals and thugs taking advantage of the police's weakened state. This group were paying very close attention to an inner-city kindergarten. There were five of them, and they kept walking past the kindergarten, looking in but not stopping. Action Man had a few moments to spare while he waited for Knuck to meet him; he thought he might as well deal with this bunch.

The leader of the gang gave a nod, and they all put on balaclavas. They were swaggering around as if they owned the street.

They were in for a nasty shock.

With a quick clap of his hands, the leader of the gang ran into the kindergarten. The others followed. A few minutes later, teachers and children ran screaming from the building and were herded by the criminals into the middle of the street. Young children were crying and running everywhere, the criminals desperately trying to keep them in order. The more they shouted, the crazier the children became. It was a total mess.

Too easy, thought Action Man, as he positioned himself behind the group of screaming children, teachers and criminals. He zeroed in on the smallest gang member, taking him out with a deft touch to the base of his neck. The thug went down like a sack of potatoes. One down, four to go, said Action Man to himself. Number two went "night-night" quicker than number one, and was soon slumbering next to his buddie.

Number three proved to be slightly trickier; he tried to punch Action Man, but his swing was too wild and too slow. Action Man used the momentum of his flailing arm to swing him around on the spot before sitting him on the ground.

"Good night," whispered Action Man into his ear, before sending the thug to join his buddies in slumberland.

With only two gang members left, the children and teachers were harder to control.

"What's happening?!" screamed the leader. "Keep 'em in line."

The only other remaining gang member tried his best, but soon he too was out for the count.

"Everyone stay calm!" screamed the leader, sounding like he was panicking, "and you won't get hurt. We're just after the ransom money!"

He waved to where he thought his third accomplice was and shouted, "Bugs! Get the truck!" But Bugs didn't respond.

"Bugs! Where are you?! Answer me! Mickey! Bruno! What's going on here?!"

"They had an urgent appointment elsewhere,"

whispered Action Man into the leader's ear. He swung around and pointed his gun at where he thought Action Man was, but there was no-one there.

"Where are you?!" he screamed, swinging this way and that. He was no match for Action Man's lightning-quick reflexes. Eventually Action Man tired of playing with him, and put him to sleep, using the same technique he had on his buddies.

It was all over in a matter of minutes. Some of the children were still upset and the teachers were comforting them, but others were playing cheerfully, practising the "sleep" hold that Action Man had used.

"Do it again," said a young girl, but he only smiled.

"I only use it on bad people," he said.

The children gathered around him, pulling at his clothes and all talking at once. Action Man crouched down to be at their height, answering their questions when he could understand them.

Action Man suddenly had a premonition of trouble. He stood quickly and herded the children off the street.

"What's the matter?" asked one of the teachers.

Action Man was about to answer when another

teacher screamed. He looked up to see an enormous concrete construction block dangling over their heads. It was suspended from a thin chain attached to a crane. This was no accident; someone had deliberately moved it there. But who? Not those pathetic criminals; this sort of menace was way out of their league.

"Move the children fast!" barked Action Man, as the concrete block jerked perilously above their heads.

Some of the youngest children started screaming again and began running around. Action Man swooped to pick them up. He heard a teacher yell "It's falling!" and looked up to see the massive concrete block hurtling towards them. Then, in an instant, it shattered into a thousand pieces above their heads and disintegrated.

A faint, mad laugh rang out from the rooftops.

Action Man was the only one who heard it, and his blood ran cold.

THE SECRET WEAPON

Action Man looked around at the tiny children—
some dazed, some clutching each other—and
breathed a sigh of relief. A small boy walked over
and held out his arms. Action Man picked him up.

"How did you make it go away?" asked the boy.

"I think I had some help," smiled Action Man.

The boy flung his arms around Action Man's neck
and the hero had a strange sensation of having done
this before. The feeling vanished when he heard the
booming voice of Knuck Williams: "That was a close
call!"

Action Man placed the boy in a policeman's arms
and walked over to where Knuck and Natalie were
sitting in the jeep. There was a strange-looking
weapon mounted on the back of the jeep. Action Man
now knew how the concrete block had miraculously
exploded into thin air.

"So you found it," he said to Knuck, who was
grinning from ear to ear.

"Right where you said it would be."

"Would someone please tell me what's going on?"
asked Natalie. She had arrived in time to see Knuck

fire this strange weapon at the lethal block of concrete, and was impressed with its power.

"I sent Knuck back to the alley where I had the close encounter last night," said Action Man.

"Told me to look for a lost 'toy,'" added Knuck. "And you know, Action Man, you were right. It was on one of the roofs."

"This is how Doctor X is destroying the buildings," said Action Man.

"What is it?' asked Natalie.

"Don't know yet," said Knuck. 'But I aim to find out fast."

Action Man told them about the laugh he had heard.

"Doctor X," whispered Natalie.

"I'm concerned that he's paying Team X-Treme too much attention," said Action Man. "Last night's attack on me, this block of concrete. From now on, let's all be extra careful."

"Jacques," said Natalie. "He's on his own back at the command centre."

"Better make contact," said Action Man.

They called Jacques and he appeared on a tiny computer screen attached to the dash of the jeep. He looked worried.

"Is everything all right?" asked Action Man.

"Well. . .I'm not sure," said Jacques. "I encountered a strange presence in the electricity grid. Someone else was in there with me, which means they know I'm looking at the power system."

Action Man told Jacques about the attacks. "Better stay out of cyberspace for a while, Jacques," he said. "They may be able to track you down."

"They'd have to be good," grinned the boy. "I've put triple and quadruple blinds around me."

"But if it's Doctor X, Jacques," said Natalie, "he might break the codes."

"Yeah, I know," said the boy impatiently. "Trust me, I'll be okay. Did you want anything else?"

"Knuck's got a toy for you to look at," said Action Man. "See if the two of you can work out how it's powered."

"Sounds like fun; when do we play?"

"This is not a game," said Knuck gruffly.

"It's not?" laughed Jacques. "Then how come I'm having so much fun?"

Action Man shook his head; sometimes he forgot

Jacques was only sixteen.

"We'll be over in five minutes," said Knuck, still stern. "Make sure you have the equipment ready."

"Yes, sir," said Jacques, saluting wildly.

His image suddenly became distorted, and then the screen went blank.

"Jacques?" said Action Man.

"Could just be a malfunction," said Natalie.

"Get over there, fast," ordered Action Man.

"What about you?" asked Natalie.

"I've got other work to do."

He jumped from the jeep and ran into the milling crowd, vanishing from view.

As Knuck swung the jeep around and sped towards the command centre, Natalie wondered for the millionth time about her boss. What sort of man was he, this Action Man?

A DISCOVERY

In the still of night, the dark figure of Action Man crept slowly up the side of a building. Dressed in his night-creeper guise, he used powerful suction pads to make his way up the building. It took tremendous effort to move his weight up the tall tower, and although he'd had little sleep over the past three days, his strong body was still capable of the effort. It had to be. He had to find Jacques—before it was too late. Knuck and Natalie had confirmed by radio what Action Man feared the most—Jacques was missing, kidnapped by X's men.

The answers seemed to lie among the clouds in the great city, on the rooftops of the mighty skyscrapers. That was where the attack had come from the other night; that was where Action Man was headed now. He wanted to make sure that Doctor X and his men would not spot his movements this time, so he climbed the side of the building instead of taking the lift.

When he reached the top, Action Man rolled over onto his feet and took out his night-scope binoculars to scan the skyline. All seemed quiet to the east; it was the same to the north and the west, but as soon as he turned the night-scopes south he saw what he was after: a faint, red glow, about half a kilometre away. The buildings were close together here, in some places almost touching each other. Action Man fired a rope over to the next building, pulled it tight and secured it. Swinging over onto his back, he made his way across the divide along the rope, leaning back to gain an upside-down view of the approaching wall. Straining to twist his body around, Action Man climbed over onto the rooftop and ran to the next building. The next gap he could easily leap, so he wasted no time in getting across. He was now two buildings away from where he had spotted the red glow.

Crouched behind an advertising sign, he could see Doctor X's skullmen scurrying around like rats on top of a glass skyscraper. Mounted near the edge of the building's roof was a giant version of the gun Knuck had recovered earlier that day. The skullmen were carefully aiming the gun towards the ground and, in a flash, Action Man realised how they did it. By firing at the base of a building they could melt its foundations. That was what caused the burning smell and the molten pool at the bottom of the crater.

Action Man looked over at the building they were aiming at. It was a government centre, which fitted X's plan to bring Centropolis to its knees. There seemed to be some activity going on at the base of the target building. Action Man adjusted his night-scopes to get a better view. Several skullmen tied something to the base of the building and then moved away quickly.

Action Man gasped as he realised it was Jacques they were tying to the building. Strapped into his wheelchair, he was helpless.

Action Man attached a long rope to a railing and threw the rest down. He launched off the side of the building, abseiling head-first at thirty kilometres an hour. This was faster than he would normally descend, but he had no choice. Halfway down, he felt a tug on the rope, then disaster struck. The rope went slack and Action Man began plummeting at a sickening speed towards the ground. Even in extreme danger, he was able to think at lightning speed. He pulled at a cord on his accessory belt and a small hook and wire fired out from an explosive bolt. The hook caught hold of a window frame, pulling Action Man up with bone-crunching force. He slammed against the side of the building, once, twice, three times, with a force that would have killed an ordinary man. Finally the swinging stopped and Action Man kicked his way in through a window and quickly disentangled himself from the hook and wire. He ran down the building's stairwell to the ground floor, kicked the front door open and was out onto the street.

"Over here!" cried Jacques, and Action Man rushed over.

He released the boy, telling him to move out fast. Now Action Man used his night-creeper suction pads to scale the glass tower. Doctor X wasn't going to get away with destroying another building, not with Action Man on the job.

At the top of the building, all was ready for the firing sequence to take place. The team leader gave the order for power-up to commence and the red sheen around the gun became brighter, then glowed white. Just as it was approaching terminal heat, Action Man reached the top of the skyscraper and rolled over the edge, scattering skullmen like skittles.

Chaos broke out: skullmen began running in all directions, as the team leader barked at them to maintain the firing sequence. Action Man launched himself at full speed towards the leader, bringing the skullman down with his momentum. He then rolled onto his front, dove under the gun and placed a small limpet mine at its base. Skullmen ran in from every direction, trying to pull Action Man from the base of the gun. But he was too fast for them and had already shot out the other side. One of the skullmen yelled a warning that there was a live mine and the villains scattered. A small, yellow explosion pushed the gun off its course, causing it to loll clumsily to one side.

The skullmen rallied now, leaping at Action Man from every side. Disorganised and unprepared, they were no match for Action Man. He used their weight and speed to swing them wildly, forcing them to crash into one another. Skullmen went down everywhere, until the team leader revived and shouted, "The gun's about to fire! Get out of here!"

Like rats deserting a sinking ship, the skullmen scampered over the side of the building, as the gun lurched perilously this way, then that. It gave a shudder before reaching terminal heat, and then fired a searing, white-hot ray straight down into the glass tower. The effect was devastating: shards of metal and molten glass shot out in every direction. Action Man covered his head as the glass tower, weakened by the gun's ray, began to sway.

There was a tremendous groan, followed by a ripping sound, as the tower crashed downward, taking Action Man with it.

MISSING IN ACTION

Natalie found Jacques, dazed and weary, in a small side street. He told her about the rescue. She called Knuck, then rushed to the spot. She was trying to locate Action Man on his emergency call signal, but he wasn't answering. Where was he?

Natalie called every five minutes, and by the time they'd reached the collapsed building, she knew something was wrong. Action Man would have answered the emergency call signal right away, unless he was in trouble. . .or injured.

Knuck arrived and he and Natalie quickly scrambled over the wreckage of the broken skyscraper.

"This one's different to the others," said Knuck. "It hasn't gone down as neatly."

"Maybe they didn't finish the job properly," said Natalie.

"Could be that Action Man stopped them, but where is he now?"

Jacques wheeled over to where they were inspecting the damage and called out, "This is the wrong building."

"What?" said Knuck.

"It's the wrong building. They meant to bring down the one behind me," he insisted.

"We haven't got time for jokes," snapped Natalie.

"It's not a joke," yelled Jacques. "They strapped me to that building over there. That was the one they were going to fire at, not this tower. The skullmen must have made a mistake."

"So they made a mistake," said Knuck impatiently, "how does that help us find Action Man?"

"Maybe it does," said Natalie.

"How might that be?" asked Knuck, as they climbed down to the ground.

"Well," said Natalie, "what if it wasn't a mistake? What if they were going to bring down this other building, but something, or someone, spoilt their plans?"

"Action Man," said Knuck.

"The gun," gasped Jacques. "It must have been mounted on top of this skyscraper."

"Of course," said Natalie. "So when Action Man arrived on the scene, it somehow fired off course and brought this skyscraper down instead."

"Do you know what you're saying?" said Knuck,

staring hard into Natalie's eyes. "If the gun misfired, then whoever was on top of that building went down with it."

"Action Man," whispered Natalie.

"Call emergency services straight away!" barked Knuck.

There was no time to lose.

Action Man felt around in the cramped, dark space; there was rubble all around him. He reached into his accessory belt and pulled out his powerful mini-torch.

He saw that he was completely covered by the fallen building; there were no cracks of light, which meant no air holes. There was probably only enough air to last him an hour; he had to find a way out.

His only hope was if he was near the top of the rubble pile, or close to its edge. If he was at the bottom, they couldn't possibly reach him in time. He decided to test the structure around him, to see if he could move it. Using all his strength, he managed to move a large, wooden board away, but instantly piles of cracked concrete and plaster started to rain down on him. It was too unstable to move this way; the whole lot could collapse. He sat back, conserving his energy, and waited.

The needle on the ultra-sensitive listening device remained still, and Natalie sighed. She poked the sensor down through another hole in the rubble and held her breath.

Please let there be something this time, she muttered to herself.

The needle flickered slightly, so slightly that Natalie almost missed it. She watched again, and for minutes nothing happened, then the needle moved again. There was no mistaking it this time, someone or something was down there. She called Knuck on his communicator.

"I think I've got something," said Natalie breathlessly.

"A sound?"

"Yes."

"I'm on my way over with plastic explosives," called Knuck, and he signed off.

Natalie shook her head, she wasn't sure that explosives were such a good idea. What if the whole structure was unstable, it could collapse in on Action Man, if indeed that was Action Man down there. If only she could be sure. Then she slapped herself on the forehead. "What an idiot," she cried.

She pulled out her communicator and set it for Action Man's call signal. If it was Action Man the sensor had picked up, then he would hear her on the communicator.

"Action Man?" she called. "Can you hear me? It's Natalie."

There was a short burst of crackle, then a faint voice replied, "I hear you."

"Action Man! Are you all right?"

"It's a bit hard to tell. There are only minor injuries I think."

"Knuck is on his way over to blast you out."

"No!" shouted Action Man down the communicator. "He mustn't do that. I repeat, do not use explosives. The situation is too unstable."

"But how will we get you out?"

"You don't have to," said Action Man. Then the line went dead.

A NEW ENEMY

Action Man lay in his dark, rubble prison, thinking calmly about finding a way out. It was obvious they couldn't blast him out, and he wouldn't get anywhere by trying to tear the wall of debris away. No, he had to be very slow and subtle about this. He had to use cunning and brains instead of force. It was simply a case of outwitting the enemy, which in this instance wasn't skullmen or criminals, but a pile of unstable rubble that could crush him like a feather. Still, the idea was the same; with cunning and a bit of skill he should be able to work his way out.

With his torch clamped firmly between his teeth, Action Man worked away at the rubble to his left. He could tell from listening carefully that this was where the wall of glass and concrete was at its thinnest. That meant it would be the shortest way to the outside, and freedom. He carefully peeled away piece after piece of rubble, placed them behind him, then inched his way forward into the gap he had created.

After nearly an hour of back-breaking work, scratching and clawing away at the broken building, he finally broke through to the surface. The sunlight was blinding, and Action Man blinked rapidly as the rush of fresh, clean air filled his lungs. He tried to make the hole big enough to crawl through, but the rubble threatened to collapse again and close off the exit forever. The hole was only centimetres wide, but it would have to do.

Action Man slowly squeezed through the gap, changing his position little by little to fit the shape of the hole. It took a tremendous effort and the sweat was pouring from his face and body. After another hour he had managed to work his head, arms and shoulders through. That would do. With great care, he flipped his communicator on and told Natalie and Knuck where they could find him.

Then he closed his eyes and rested, knowing that in a few hours he would be back fighting the real enemy—Doctor X.

THE X-LASER

It didn't take long for Natalie and Knuck to free Action Man from the rubble. They wanted to take him to a hospital for a check-up but he refused. There was still important work to do, and he couldn't afford to waste time seeing what damage had been done to his body; he would just have to trust that it would be okay. He called Team X-Treme together, and sat back to hear what they had to report.

"Jacques," he said, "did you find out anything about the power grid before you were kidnapped?"

"Well," said Jacques slowly, "whatever this heat, melting gun thing is, it uses up an enormous amount of electrical power. More than the whole of Centropolis would use in one day."

"So how can they fire it without blacking out the city?" asked Natalie.

"That's the most incredible part," smiled Jacques, leaning forward in his chair. "They don't just take it from Centropolis. When I was in the grid, VR-style. . ."

"V what?" boomed Knuck.

"VR," replied Jacques. "Virtual reality. When I was in there, I encountered a few sentries. . ."

"You mean there were other people in the computer system with you?" exclaimed Knuck.

"Well, not exactly," said Jacques. "You see, VR doesn't mean you're actually in the computer, just your electronic image is. I'm still in my chair with my laptop, but by using certain commands, I can explore the system."

"So, these sentries," said Action Man, "they were put there by Doctor X?"

"No doubt about it," said Jacques. "They were there to stop anyone finding out how he's drawing the electrical power."

"How did you get past them?" asked Natalie.

"By answering a riddle," he answered.

"Oh now, come on!" boomed Knuck. "This isn't a joke."

"It's true," explained Jacques. "I answered a riddle to get past the sentry, but that's how X's men were able to track me down. To answer the riddle, I had to drop my double and triple blinds. Don't you get it?"

"No I don't," said Knuck, shaking his head.

Action Man stepped in before Jacques could explain what double and triple blinds were. The boy was a genius when it came to computers, but right now they needed straight answers.

"The power, Jacques," said Action Man. "How is he getting it?"

"Simple," replied Jacques. "He draws it from around the world. A little from New York, a little from Sydney, a little from London. No-one notices it's gone that way. It's very sophisticated actually."

Action Man turned to Knuck and asked him for a report on the gun.

"Well," said Knuck. "As far as I can tell it's some sort of laser, but it's more powerful than any I've ever seen. Just look at the way it melted the foundations of those buildings. I mean, some of those foundations go down hundreds of metres. This laser thing. . . whatever you want to call it. . ."

"X-Laser," suggested Jacques.

"That's good," said Knuck. "You can bet the bank that Doctor X has plenty more of them. And they are going to take a lot of stopping. Just look at what happened to Action Man when he tried last night."

"Not necessarily," said Natalie. "Not if we beat him at his own game."

She smiled, and Team X-Treme gathered closer to hear what she had in mind.

DOCTOR X'S MESSAGE

Doctor X stood on the roof of the trade centre and surveyed the damaged skyline of Centropolis. From his vantage point, he could see the entire city; there were ugly craters everywhere. Doctor X smiled at the destruction he had brought upon this once-magnificent city.

"Soon there will be nothing left," he said to no-one in particular. Then he smiled and sighed with satisfaction.

He moved his massive, twisted body towards the centre of the rooftop. He had been broken and put together so many times by the demented doctors who pledged loyalty to his wicked cause that there was very little of his original body left. He had artificial arms that were operated by a sophisticated form of hydraulics, and his body was ten times stronger than any normal man's.

Behind him, his top crew were working on the largest X-Laser gun of them all. It had the capacity to bring down a building up to twenty kilometres away. Tonight, Doctor X would send a terrifying message to the world; with this gun he would wipe out the whole of Centropolis. The only building left standing after his long night of destruction would be this trade centre.

Once the governments of the world saw the awesome capacity of the X-Laser gun, they would give in to any demand he made of them. And if they didn't, he would bring their cities down as well. What could possibly stop him now? Not that pathetic Team X-Treme; they were in tatters, their leader entombed in the shattered glass tower. Doctor X's only regret was that he hadn't killed Action Man personally. He shrugged his shoulders; what did it matter anyway? Action Man was dead and any hopes the world had of stopping the X-Laser gun had died with him.

The red glow surrounding the X-Laser gun started to build in intensity, growing brighter and brighter as it moved towards terminal heat. A massive amount of power, stolen from the major electricity grids of the world, was being sucked into Doctor X's evil gun of destruction.

"Perfect," whispered Doctor X, as he watched the gun grow hotter.

The team leader checked the gun's instrument

panel and scratched his head.

"It should be reaching fifty per cent by now," he shouted to the skullman behind him.

The skullman scurried back to his computer and typed a few commands, then shook his head.

"I don't understand it," he said to the team leader. "According to the program, we *are* pulling fifty per cent."

"Well, where in blazes is it?!" shouted the leader.

Doctor X looked over at his henchmen and frowned. Nothing was going to spoil his party tonight. He marched over to the team leader and demanded that he produce the necessary power.

"Now!" shouted Doctor X. "Or I'll feed you to my pet sharks."

The team leader pushed the computer skullman away and started typing furiously at the keyboard. His attempts were useless; every command he typed was cancelled by Jacques, who was operating from inside the computer. He had fooled the computer into believing it was drawing the power. Jacques was in command, and when the time was right, he would release the juice in one big bang.

"I don't understand it, sir," said the leader nervously.

"The program says that power is gaining every minute. We should be reaching terminal heat. . ."

"You fool!" shouted Doctor X. "The gun is cooling down, not heating up. Someone has sabotaged your computer!"

"But. . .who?" asked the team leader.

The answer to his question came straight away. From the east, the faint sound of a helicopter broke the still night air. It grew and grew until the chopper was hovering menacingly above them.

"Action Man!" screamed Doctor X when he saw the hero at the chopper door. "You're meant to be dead!"

"Sorry to disappoint you," shouted Action Man to his enemy.

Suddenly another chopper appeared. This one was carrying a huge sheet of polished steel, attached to it by cable. Knuck piloted this chopper, manoeuvring the sheet of polished steel to a position twenty metres in front of the gun.

Doctor X laughed. "You fools!" he shouted, "My gun will melt that steel in seconds."

Just then, the X-Laser gun jolted into life, growing brighter and brighter until it was glowing white-hot. Jacques had released just enough power to send out a current.

"Power's up, sir," shouted the team leader.

The gun gave off a short warning signal before the deadly red ray shot from its nozzle. The X-Laser hit the steel sheet and was immediately sent back. With the power weakened by Jacques, the ray wasn't strong enough to cut through the steel. It bounced straight off the highly polished surface, just like torch light bouncing off a mirror. The mighty X-Laser gun boiled for a few seconds as it destroyed itself. There was a tremendous explosion that sent white-hot metal shooting in every direction, then all was silent.

All that was left of Doctor X's evil X-Laser gun was a pool of molten metal.

Action Man gave a shout and the two choppers landed. Within seconds, Team X-Treme were creating havoc amongst the skullmen.

X ESCAPES

The skullmen outnumbered Team X-Treme by twenty to one, and yet the odds were against them. Doctor X's evil crew were no match for Knuck's sheer strength and courage. He could take two men on at a time, then turn and drop to one knee to throw a third man over his shoulder. Behind Knuck, Natalie was giving lessons in the martial arts; with her rapid-fire movements she was knocking skullmen senseless before they knew what hit them. And, of course, there was also Action Man. He employed his subtle form of fighting, using a rolling movement to add to his opponents' momentum and send them flying through the air.

Doctor X quickly realised that it was time for drastic measures. He climbed to the top of a huge neon sign that blinked red and blue above the battle. It stood ten metres high and must have weighed at least a tonne. It was held steady by guide cables, which the evil doctor cut through with machine-gun fire. Doctor X climbed down from the sign, which was now swaying dangerously. He fired at its base until the sign was almost completely severed from its moorings.

Action Man saw what he was up to and called out to Knuck and Natalie. They jumped out of the way, as the sign came crashing down and knocked one of the choppers over the side of the building. Electrical sparks flew everywhere as the sign exploded.

In the confusion, Doctor X ran to the remaining chopper and climbed in. He fired up the engine, then pulled back on the joystick. The huge rotors strained to take the extra weight of the polished steel sheet. Doctor X cursed; he'd knocked the wrong chopper off the building.

Action Man quickly scrambled onto the shoulders of a bewildered skullman. He leapt onto the steel sheet, clinging with all his might to its edge, as the chopper swung out into the night sky. Doctor X took the chopper higher and higher, away from the rooftops. Action Man scrambled up the edge of the steel sheet. He reached the top, made his way along the thick cable and climbed into the cargo bay of the helicopter.

"It's a shame you had to leave so soon, Doctor X," said Action Man, as he scrambled into the cockpit.

"Action Man!" shouted the doctor. "What a surprise.

Did you forget your hat or something?"

"I don't think so," said Action Man, lunging at his enemy.

The helicopter lurched violently as Action Man wrenched Doctor X from the controls, pulling him into the cargo area. The two men struggled wildly. One used electronic and mechanical strength, his twisted body more machine than human; the other relied on natural strength, and skills developed in a past he couldn't remember.

Doctor X pulled a fire hydrant from the wall and brought it crashing down onto Action Man's head. The hero lay dazed, as Doctor X scrambled back into the cockpit and righted the lurching chopper.

Action Man came to and dived full-length at the doctor, throwing both arms around his twisted neck. Doctor X fought against Action Man, trying to control the flight path of the helicopter. He pulled the joystick left, towards the heart of the city, and Action Man strained to pull it back again, out towards the ocean. He didn't want Doctor X in control of this lethal machine over the population of Centropolis. There was nothing this madman wouldn't do.

The two men struggled to gain control of the chopper, as it edged closer and closer towards the sea. They passed over a football field and Doctor X squared the joystick, causing the helicopter to hover above the crowded stadium. There it sat, with its enormous load of steel sheeting swaying over the mass of people below.

"Now, my little Action Man," sneered X, "you be a good boy and leave this helicopter. Otherwise, I might accidentally slip and drop this sheet of steel on all those innocent sports fans."

"You scum," hissed Action Man.

"Now now, let's keep it polite," hissed Doctor X. "You never did have any manners. Oh, but I forgot, you don't know about that, do you? Only I do." He laughed a wicked laugh that sent shivers down Action Man's spine.

"You'd love to know, wouldn't you? You snivelling little Action Man. You'd love to know about your worthless life."

Action Man moved slightly closer to X, hoping to gain a vantage point from which to attack.

"Stay right there, thank you," smiled Doctor X. "It's a shame you'll have to die without ever knowing your past, isn't it?"

Action Man looked down at the crowded stadium. He had no doubt that X would release the sheet of steel. Hundreds of people would be injured or killed. He had no option; he had to jump out of the chopper.

Action Man went over to the door and closed his eyes momentarily, then turned to his enemy.

"This isn't over yet," he hissed.

"It is for you," sneered X. "Get out!"

Action Man leapt from the chopper, the evil laugh of Doctor X ringing in his ears.

The chopper soared higher and higher into the night sky, gaining speed at a rapid rate. In the cockpit, Doctor X searched for the switch that would release the steel sheet.

What a fool that Action Man is, he thought, as he searched the instrument panel. Giving his life for a miserable bunch of people he didn't even know.

When he at last found the switch, he laughed aloud and shouted, "I'll drop it on them anyway. It'll be my tribute to the pathetic life of Action Man!"

Doctor X paused to enjoy the moment. He wished there could be music, some sort of fanfare to mark the occasion. As he reached for the switch, a black-gloved hand grabbed his twisted arm in a vice-like grip.

"Actually," hissed Action Man in his ear, "you are the pathetic one."

Doctor X swung his mechanical arm up and caught Action Man around the neck, pulling back with massive force. It was all Action Man could do to keep his balance against the unnatural "strength" of the doctor's arm. He braced himself against the cockpit's instrument panel, then reached out for the joystick, pushing it forward violently. The chopper lurched downward and both the doctor and Action Man were thrown against the windshield of the cockpit.

Action Man recovered quickly, rolling away from the instrument panel and pulling the joystick back again. As the chopper righted itself, Action Man threw a steel cable around the doctor's legs and attached it to the cargo bay door. He tightened it round the thrashing doctor a few times until he was immobilised.

"You just stay there for a while," said Action Man. "I've got work to do."

He pulled the chopper out to the east, flying low and fast across the city, until he reached the ocean. When he was a few kilometres from the coast, Action Man released the steel sheet. It fell into the sea with a mighty splash, the white spray glinting in the moonlight.

Now that the chopper was light and easy to manoeuvre, Action Man flew it back towards Centropolis and the Team X-Treme rendezvous point. He was about to turn towards the doctor to see if he was still secure, when his sixth sense warned him of danger.

Action Man rolled away from the pilot's seat, as a deadly stream of X-Laser hit the instrument panel. Doctor X laughed wildly, a tiny X-Laser gun smoking in his hand. He aimed it at the steel cable wrapped around his legs, and cut through it like a scissor through silk. He aimed the gun at Action Man, who pushed back onto his shoulders, then launched himself forward, bringing his head up into his enemy's stomach. Doctor X let out a huge groan, as he was pushed a metre into the air.

"Still playing with toys," said Action Man grimly, flicking the X-Laser gun from the doctor's hand. It flew through the air, spinning towards the open cargo bay door.

Doctor X lunged for the gun but was too late; it fell out into the night sky and down into the sea. At that moment, the chopper dropped dangerously, slewing to one side as it veered out of control.

Action Man looked over at the instrument panel, which was a mess of fried electronics and cables. This helicopter was going down. The best he could do was make sure that Doctor X didn't escape before it hit the sea. Activating the emergency beacon on his accessory belt, Action Man wrapped his powerful legs around the doctor's middle.

"Let go of me, you freak!" yelled Doctor X, struggling in vain.

They could see the ocean spinning towards them, as the chopper plummeted downward.

"Goodbye, doctor," said Action Man. "It hasn't been nice knowing you."

"How would you know?" laughed Doctor X.

MISSION ACCOMPLISHED

Action Man awoke to the blurry image of Natalie Poole looking down at him. He blinked his eyes a few times, but she remained out of focus.

"He's awake," whispered Natalie to someone behind her.

Knuck Williams' face came into view, then all went black.

Action Man was swimming through thick, black oil. The harder he pushed, the thicker the oil became, until he was trapped by the pressure. He opened his mouth to call out, but it filled with oil. . . but it wasn't oil, was it? Action Man woke again to find it was night. He started to remember the fight in the helicopter. Team X-Treme must have fished me out of the sea, he thought. He moved his arms and legs; they felt okay. He tried speaking.

"Hello," he croaked.

Natalie came into view again, followed by Jacques and Knuck. They had all been waiting in his room.

"How are you feeling?" asked Natalie.

"Well, there's someone banging nails inside my head," said Action Man in a hoarse whisper.

"I'm not surprised," grinned Knuck. "You would have hit that water at high speed."

"We found you soon after, thanks to your emergency beacon," added Jacques.

"Doctor X?" asked Action Man.

Natalie shook her head and Knuck looked grim.

"No sign, I'm afraid," said Knuck. "He might have gone down to the bottom. . ."

"Or he might have escaped," said Action Man. "Doctor X has an amazing ability to survive."

"I'm sure he'll let us know if he's still around," said Natalie.

"There is some good news," said Knuck. "We managed to analyse the X-Laser."

"Uses a special chip made from a rare crystal," added Jacques.

"And guess who has locked up all known supplies of the crystal," smiled Natalie.

"Well done," smiled Action Man.

If X was still alive, at least he wouldn't be using his deadly X-Laser any more. But Action Man was sure it wouldn't be long before X came up with another sick plan. Deep in his heart, Action Man knew that X would have survived the crash. He knew that the fight wasn't over yet.

With a deep sigh, Action Man closed his eyes—he had to rest and recover. The day would come when Team X-Treme would be called upon once more, and he would be there to lead them.